ALI THE GREAT

Never Gives Up!

written by SAADIA FARUQI   illustrated by DEBBY RAHMALIA

PICTURE WINDOW BOOKS
a capstone imprint

For Mubashir —SF
For Alesha —DR

Published by Picture Window Books, an imprint of Capstone
1710 Roe Crest Drive
North Mankato, Minnesota 56003
capstonepub.com

Text copyright © 2025 by Saadia Faruqi.
Illustrations copyright © 2025 by Capstone.

All rights reserved. No part of this publication may be reproduced in whole or in part, or stored in a retrieval system, or transmitted in any form or by any means, electronic, mechanical, photocopying, recording, or otherwise, without written permission of the publisher.

Library of Congress Cataloging-in-Publication Data is available on the Library of Congress website.

ISBN: 9780756594107 (paperback)
ISBN: 9780756594114 (ebook PDF)

Summary: Ali Tahir is back with four more stories! This Pakistani American second grader likes to be the hero. But when things go wrong, Ali keeps trying and relies on his friends and family for help. Whether he's cooking with Dadi, building a robot, or doing magic tricks for show-and-tell, a hero sometimes needs backup! In this collection of clever stories, discover how Ali never gives up his quest for greatness!

Designers: Kay Fraser and Tracy Davies

Any additional websites and resources referenced in this book are not maintained, authorized, or sponsored by Capstone. All product and company names are trademarks™ or registered® trademarks of their respective holders.

TABLE OF CONTENTS

ALI THE GREAT
AND THE BUG HUNT HAZARD ............ 6

ALI THE GREAT
AND THE ROBOT MELTDOWN ........28

ALI THE GREAT
AND THE MAGIC TRICK FIX ......... 50

ALI THE GREAT
AND TOO MANY COOKS .................. 72

LET'S LEARN SOME URDU!

Ali and his family speak both English and Urdu, a language from Pakistan. Now you'll know some Urdu too!

ABBA (ah-BAH)—father (also baba)

AMMA (ah-MAH)—mother (also mama)

BHAI (BHA-ee)—brother

DADA (DAH-dah)—grandfather on father's side

DADI (DAH-dee)—grandmother on father's side

SALAAM (sah-LAHM)—hello

SHUKRIYA (shuh-KREE-yuh)—thank you

ALI THE GREAT
and the Bug Hunt Hazard

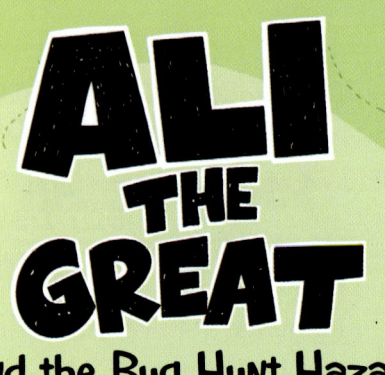

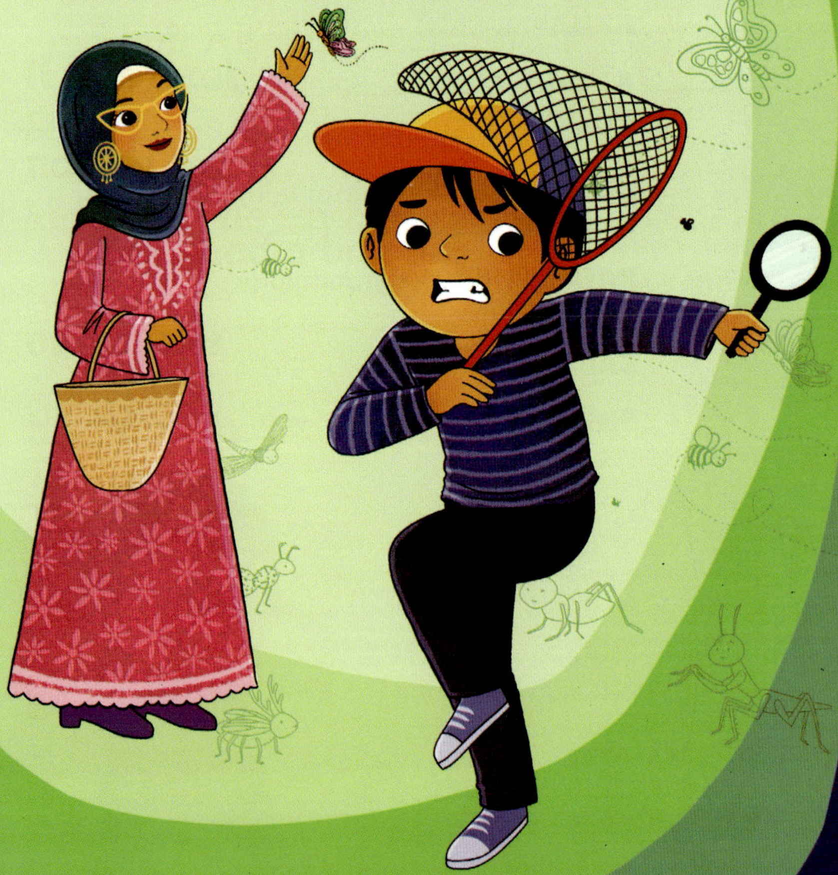

☆ Chapter 1 ☆

One Saturday morning, Amma took Ali to the park. He brought his net and magnifying glass.

"Let's hunt for bugs!" Ali said, grinning.

"The park has lots of insects for us to learn about," Amma said. She was a scientist, and she loved learning new things.

Ali waved his net around.
"Maybe I'll discover a new kind of bug!" he exclaimed. "They'll name it Ali, after me!"

"Maybe," Amma said with a smile.

Ali saw a squirrel dart across the path. He heard birds chirping. But he didn't see or hear any bugs.

Then something buzzed in Ali's ear. He jumped. "Mosquito!"

"Looks like you found your first bug," Amma said.

Ali slapped the air around him. "I don't like mosquitoes! They bite!"

"But they feed other animals," Amma said. She rubbed a special lotion over them both. "This will keep them away from us."

Ali crouched down and looked through his magnifying glass. "Just ants," he said with a sigh. "There aren't any good bugs here."

"Keep looking." Amma pointed to a big tree lying on the ground. "Check behind there."

Ali leaned over the tree and sniffed. "It's stinky!" he said.

Then he saw a pile of dog poop behind the tree. And lots of flies!

"Ew!" Ali yelled.

☆ Chapter 2 ☆

OUCH!

Amma laughed. "Flies are important too, you know."

Ali frowned. "Not the kind of bugs I'm looking for!"

Amma showed him more spots where bugs could be hiding. Behind tall grass. Under a pile of leaves.

Then Ali saw some flowers. "Maybe I'll find a ladybug," he said. "Those are my favorite!"

Ali pushed his face right into a flower, trying to smell it.

"Be careful," Amma warned. "There could be . . ."

"Ow!" Ali cried. Something had stung him right on the nose.

Amma rushed over to help. "A bee sting," she said, looking at his nose. "It's a little red, but not swollen."

Ali stomped his feet. "I hate bugs," he announced. "They're itchy and stinky and mean!"

Amma and Ali sat on a bench. She gently put some medicine on his bee sting.

"All bugs have jobs to do," she said. "So we have to be careful to stay clear of their habitat."

"What's habitat?" Ali asked.

"It's where a creature lives," Amma explained. "We have to give them space. Not stick our faces in and bother them."

"I want to go back to my habitat now," Ali said, rubbing his sore nose.

HAPPY HABITAT

Amma patted Ali's knee. "Let's try one more place."

They walked down the path to a garden. It was full of flowers, bushes, and fruit trees.

"Look, those honeybees are taking nectar to make into honey," Amma said, pointing.

Ali saw them and backed up a few steps.

Then a butterfly flew past and landed on a bright red flower. Ali smiled and tiptoed toward it. He didn't want to bother it.

"Hello, butterfly," Ali whispered.

"Every time they land on a fruit or flower, they're helping more plants to grow," Amma said.

Ali looked at his net, but then he set it down. "It looks happier on that flower," he said. "I mean, its habitat."

Amma hugged him. "Being kind to bugs is the most important part of being a bug expert."

"Bzzzz!" Ali replied.

☆ Chapter 1 ☆

A ROBOT BATTLE

Ms. Alex rolled out a big cart with lots of little drawers. "Are you ready to create?" she asked the class.

"I'm the best creator! Sign me up!" Ali cheered.

The cart was full of small bins that held all kinds of things. Some had tools like scissors, glue, and tape. Others had buttons, felt, and cardboard.

Yasmin took out a bin full of building bricks. "What's all this for?" she asked.

"It's a makerspace!" Ms. Alex explained. "You can use these supplies to make anything you like."

Emma picked up some googly eyes. "Let's make robots!" she said.

"Robots are cool!" Zack said. He pulled out some tubes and cans.

Ali's heart thumped. His friends were taking all the good supplies! He quickly grabbed what he could find as they all got to work.

"Mine will be the biggest!" Emma boasted.

"Mine will be the fastest," Zack bragged.

"Mine will look the best!" Yasmin said. "Not that it's a competition," she added.

Ali frowned. *Everything* was a competition, wasn't it? He wanted to win.

☆ Chapter 2 ☆

MELTDOWN

Soon, everyone had finished their robot. But no one was very happy.

Emma's robot was huge but lopsided. Zack's robot had wheels, but it rolled too slowly. Yasmin's robot was colorful, but it didn't do anything.

Ali thought his robot was the worst of all. It had floppy arms and a crooked body made of bent cardboard.

"These are all bad!" he said, and he kicked his robot.

It flew across the rug and crashed into Zack's robot . . .

which rolled into Emma's . . .

which fell sideways onto Yasmin's . . .

which broke into pieces.

"Oh no!" Yasmin gasped.

Ms. Alex came over. "Is there a problem, maker friends?"

Yasmin, Emma, and Zack all looked down and started to clean up.

Ali went to the corner and sat down. He felt bad. He hadn't meant to destroy his friends' robots.

"I'm sorry," he mumbled, but nobody heard him.

☆ Chapter 3 ☆

THE BEST ROBOT

Ali looked over at his friends.

Zack was busy putting his wheels back on.

Emma was using markers to add color to her robot.

Ali snapped his fingers. "We could combine our robots into one biggest, fastest, best robot!" he said.

"How?" Yasmin asked.

"By working together," Ali replied. "Like a team."

"Great idea!" Emma said. "I'll work on the body."

"I'll do the wheels!" Zack said. "I have an idea to make them roll faster."

"And I can work on the face!" Yasmin added. She held up some paintbrushes.

Ali thought about the robot. What could he do to make it even better? Big, fast . . . and *loud*!

Aha! He dug through the bins and got to work.

Soon, the robot was ready.

"Looks great!" Ms. Alex said.

"Can we see it in action?"

Ali gave the robot a push. It flew across the room on its wheels. As it rolled, the bell Ali had attached began to ring.

The robot was big. It was fast. It was loud. It was the best!

The class clapped. Ali grinned.

Good friends working together.

That was a win!

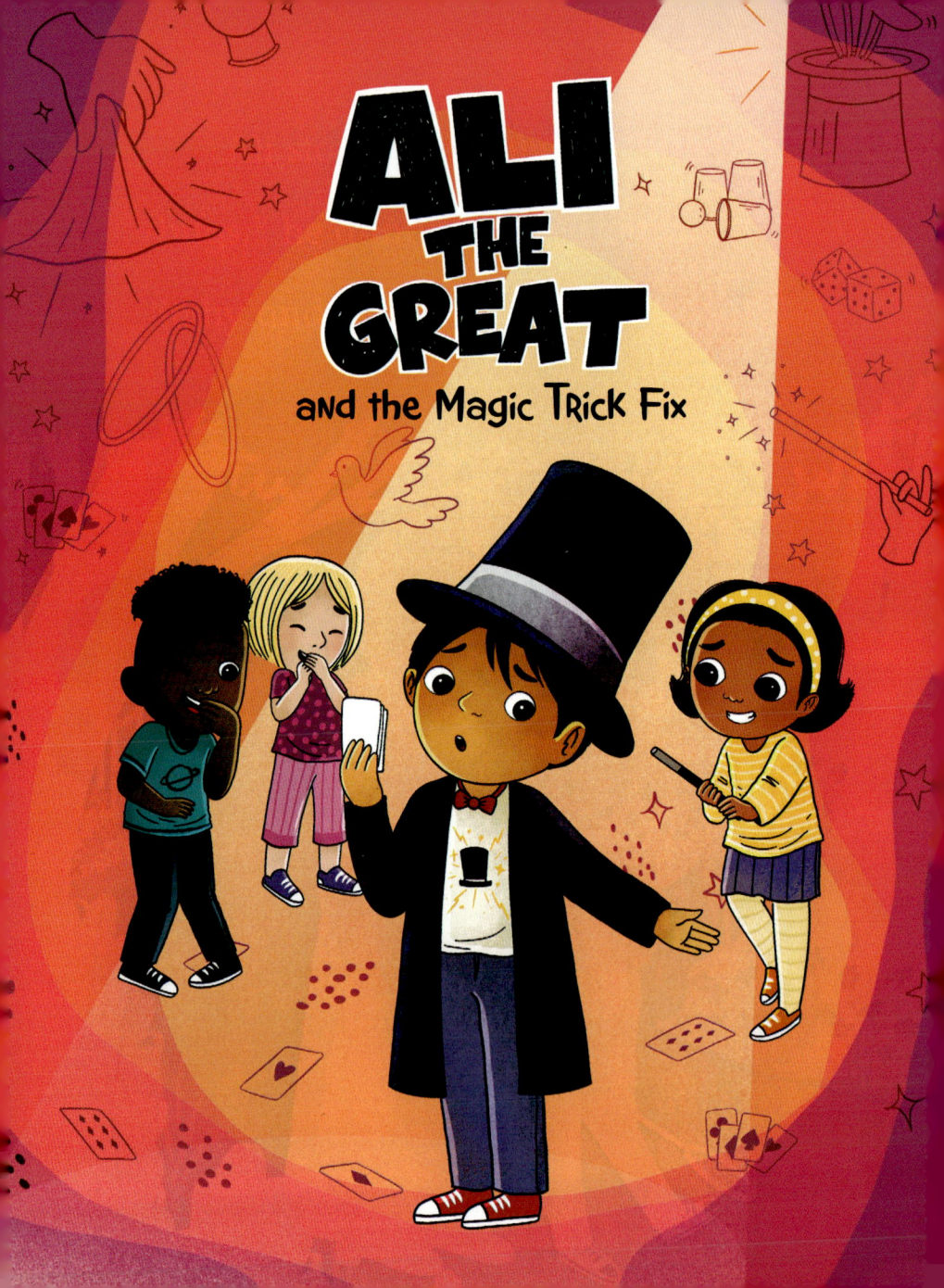

☆ Chapter 1 ☆

SHOW-AND-TELL

"Is everyone ready for show-and-tell?" Ms. Alex asked one morning.

Ali raised his hand high into the air. "Me! Me!" he yelled.

Ms. Alex raised her eyebrows.

"Students who are waiting patiently will go first," she said.

Ali frowned. Waiting patiently was hard. Especially when he had something amazing to show the class.

Yasmin went first. She'd brought a new book to share. It was all about the planets.

"Very nice, Yasmin," Ms. Alex said.

Emma was next. She showed the class her favorite stuffed animal. It was a rabbit named Hopsy.

Zack had a bag full of marbles from his grandfather. They were blue, red, yellow, and green.

Ali sighed. His friends' show-and-tell items were boring.

Finally, Ms. Alex said, "Your turn, Ali. What did you bring today?"

Ali jumped up with a little purple bag. "I can do magic tricks!" he said proudly.

"Show us!" Zack begged.

Ali opened the bag and pulled out his magic wand. Then he held up items one at a time. A rope. A deck of cards. Silver rings. Colorful napkins.

Then Ali showed his classmates a paper clip.

"I can make this disappear," he said. "It's easy peasy."

Emma clapped her hands in excitement.

"Go, Ali!" Yasmin cheered.

☆ Chapter 2 ☆

MAGIC MISTAKES

Ali held the paper clip between his fingers and flipped it.

The paper clip dropped to the floor, right in front of everyone.

Ali bit his lip.

It was supposed to stick to his thumb, not fall down in plain sight. "Oops," he mumbled.

The class giggled.

"It's okay, Ali," Ms. Alex said. "Try another one."

Ali gulped and picked up the rope. "I will magically split this into two pieces!" he announced.

He twisted the rope, then knotted it. Once, twice, three times.

Then he pulled both ends and shouted, "Ta-da!"

The rope stayed in one piece.

This time his classmates laughed loudly.

"Quiet, please," Ms. Alex said sternly.

Ali's cheeks turned pink. He quickly picked up a big green napkin. "Um, how about I make this napkin fly like a bird?"

The class watched as he tossed the napkin high into the air . . . but it just floated down to Yasmin's desk.

She picked it up and handed it back to him. "Good try, Ali," she whispered.

Ali scowled. He wished he'd never brought his tricks to school. He couldn't do a single one right. He felt like a big failure.

☆ Chapter 3 ☆

A LITTLE HELP

Yasmin raised her hand. "Maybe I could be your assistant?" she offered.

Ali frowned. He didn't need an assistant. Did he?

But he couldn't stand everyone laughing at him.

Ali nodded, and Yasmin got up and stood beside him.

"You can do it, Ali!" she whispered.

Ali took a deep breath. He picked up two silver rings that were joined together. He handed them to Yasmin.

"Can you break these apart, assistant?" he asked.

Yasmin pulled. "Nope!" she replied.

Ali took the rings back.

"Abracadabra!" He twisted the rings apart and then held them up high.

"Hooray!" The class clapped and cheered.

Yasmin looked at the rings. "How did you do that?" she whispered.

Ali smiled. "A magician never tells," he replied.

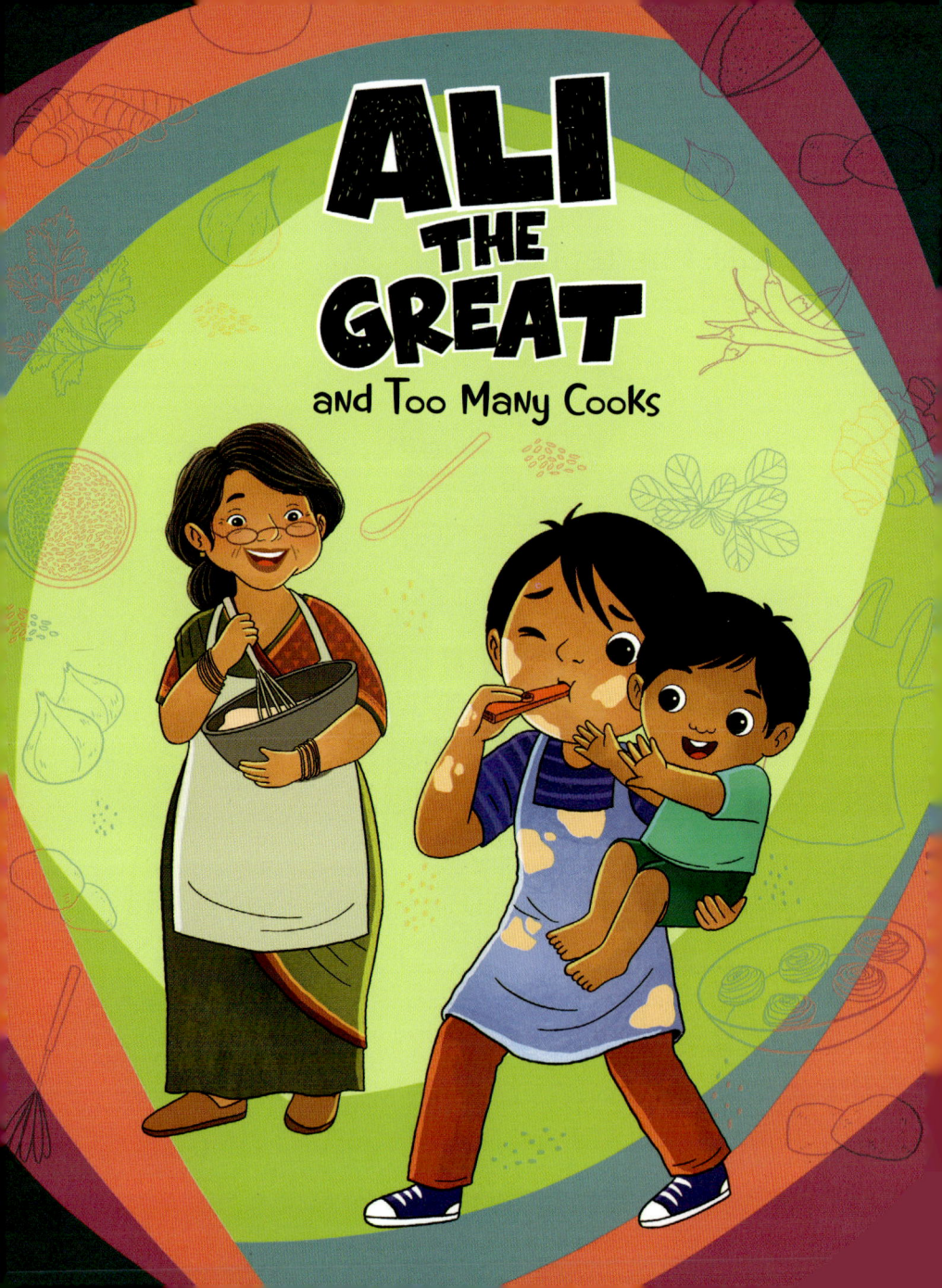

☆ Chapter 1 ☆

COZY KITCHEN

"Time to cook, Ali!" Dadi called from the kitchen.

Ali loved to cook with Dadi on the weekends. It was their fun time. What would they cook today? Samosas? Chicken curry? Roti? Maybe all of them!

"Coming, Dadi!" Ali called.

"Me too!" Fateh yelled, running after his brother.

Ali's grin faded. He knew Fateh would just get in the way. But Amma and Abba had gone shopping, and Dada was taking a nap.

"You can help too," Ali said with a sigh.

In the kitchen, he helped Fateh up onto a stool. Dadi put a big bowl, a mixing spoon, and a box of chickpea flour on the counter. Then she took cilantro and onions from the fridge.

"Can you guess what we're making?" she asked.

Ali looked at the ingredients. "Give me a hint," he begged.

Fateh puffed up his cheeks and blew in Ali's face.

"Ew, Fateh! Don't blow on me!" Ali said.

Fateh blew again, then giggled.

Ali shook his head. Maybe Fateh was too warm. He ran to Fateh's room to get a T-shirt with short sleeves.

Quickly, he helped Fateh change his shirt. Then he turned back to Dadi. "So, what are we making?"

☆ Chapter 2 ☆

MAYBE A KAZOO?

"We're making pakoras!" Dadi said.

"Yum!" Ali cheered.

They poured flour and spices into the bowl, then added water. Ali mixed the batter.

Dadi chopped up the cilantro and onion. She tossed them into the bowl. "Looks ready," she said.

Fateh slapped his hands on the counter and started blowing air again. His lips made a sputtering sound. *Ew.*

Ali frowned. Cooking time with Dadi was getting spoiled because of his little brother.

Fateh kept blowing.

Ali snapped his fingers. "I know what you want!" He ran to Fateh's room again and brought back his kazoo.

"Gimme!" Fateh cried when he saw it.

While Fateh blew into his kazoo, Ali helped Dadi cook.

Dadi heated up oil in a big pan until it was very hot. Then she dropped spoonfuls of batter into the pan. The batter sizzled as it fried.

Ali took out a platter and lined it with paper. The paper would absorb the extra oil from the pakoras.

Then Ali looked around. Something was missing. "We need ketchup!" he said.

Dadi smiled. "Can't have pakoras without ketchup," she agreed. "And don't forget some chutney for Dada."

Fateh threw his kazoo on the ground. He blew another big blast of air right in Ali's face.

Yuck!

HOT PAKORAS!

"Fateh, stop!" Ali groaned. "What's the matter with you?"

Fateh started clapping and kept on blowing slobbery air.

Ali scowled. Why couldn't he have one day without his brother annoying him?

Dadi took the sizzling pakoras out of the pan and placed them on the paper.

"Gimme!" Fateh yelled.

"Careful—they're hot," Dadi warned.

Ali plucked a pakora off the tray Dadi was carrying and blew on it.

Ali looked at his brother.

Fateh's little face was scrunched up,
blowing too. He looked so excited.

"Gimme," Fateh whispered with a huge grin.

Ali started laughing. "So *that's* what you were doing, you silly goose!" he said. He placed a pakora in front of Fateh. "Cooling down a pretend pakora, eh?"

Dadi laughed too and sat down to join them. They all blew on their hot pakoras until they were cool enough to take a bite.

Yum!

THINK BIG WITH ALI THE GREAT!

- ☆ What was a special time you spent with a parent or caretaker? Write a paragraph about a good memory with that person.

- ☆ Draw a picture of the most amazing robot you can imagine. What does it do?

- ☆ Does your class do show-and-tell? What is something you would like to show? Make a list of things you would tell your classmates about it.

- ☆ Do you like cooking or baking with your family? Draw pictures of the foods you like to make and put labels beneath them.

JUST JOKING AROUND

What did one firefly say to the other?
Gotta glow now!

What is a robot's favorite snack?
Computer chips

What kind of candy do magicians like to eat?
Twix

What day do eggs hate the most?
Fry-day!

About the Author

Saadia Faruqi is a Pakistani American writer, interfaith activist, and cultural sensitivity trainer featured in O, The Oprah Magazine. Author of the Yasmin chapter book series, Saadia also writes middle grade novels, such as *Yusuf Azeem Is Not a Hero*, and other books for children. Saadia is editor-in-chief of *Blue Minaret*, an online magazine of poetry, short stories, and art. Besides writing, she also loves reading, binge-watching her favorite shows, and taking naps. She lives in Houston with her family.

About the Illustrator

Debby Rahmalia is an illustrator based in Indonesia with a passion for storytelling. She enjoys creating diverse works that showcase an array of cultures and people. Debby's long-term dream was to become an illustrator. She was encouraged to pursue her dream after she had her first baby and has been illustrating ever since. When she's not drawing, she spends her time reading the books she illustrated to her daughter or wandering around the neighborhood with her.